NeLLY PUG GroWS MUSCLeS

NELLY PUG GROWS MUSCLES

Megan Johnson McCullough, EdD

Illustrated by Alexis Eastburn

Charleston, SC
www.PalmettoPublishing.com

Nelly Pug Grows Muscles

First Edition

Hardcover ISBN: 979-8-8229-0739-3
Paperback ISBN: 979-8-8229-0740-9

Nelly Pug is the story of Megan and her natural bodybuilding coach, Lorenzo Gaspar. To Megan, the butterfly is a symbol of her mother whom she lost to alcohol addiction. Her mother's butterfly spirit flies with her daily and has taught her to spread her wings, especially when standing on that competition stage. Megan has had pugs since she was a little girl. Her pugs (named Steve Nash and Scottie Pippen who are basketball players) are the mascots at her fitness studio, Every BODY's Fit. "Nelly" is Coach Lorenzo's mother's name and represents Megan, herself in this story. Lorenzo is Coach Eddie Monarch in this story. "Eddie" is Megan's father's middle name. Megan played basketball growing up and her father is a basketball coach. "Ryan" (Ryan Pug in this story) is her husband, Carl's middle name. Therefore, this story is dedicated to Megan's mother, Coach Lorenzo Gaspar, Megan's father, and Megan's husband, who together, are her team of non-stop support both on the stage and in life.

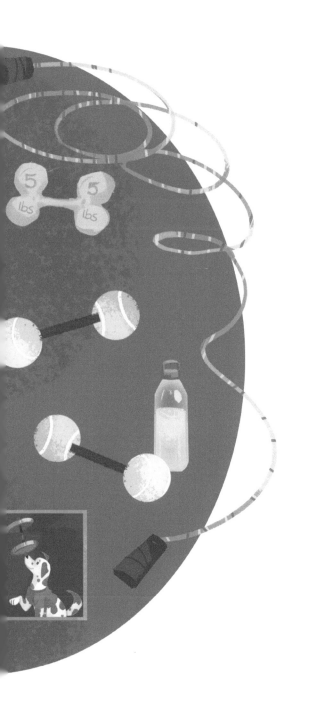

NELLY PUG

loved to exercise, especially lifting weights. She saw strong dogs at the gym and wanted to be just like them. There were pictures of the bodybuilder dogs on the walls and Nelly Pug would stare at them in amazement.

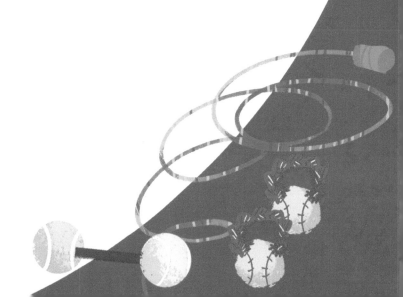

NELLY PUG

hired Coach Eddie Monarch
to help her grow muscles.

She listened to all his advice,
woke up early to train with him,
ate very healthy, and practiced
her posing every single day.

NELLY PUG

lifted weights, ate chicken,
asparagus, and sweet potatoes,
drank lots of water all the time,
and made sure to go to bed early.

Sometimes

NELLY PUG

didn't feel like exercising and wanted some ice cream, but Coach Eddie Monarch said she needed to believe in herself and her goals and stick to her game plan. He said, "Champions don't make excuses".

NELLY PUG

and Coach Eddie Monarch went to bodybuilding competitions all over the world including places like Las Vegas, Italy, South Korea, and Australia.

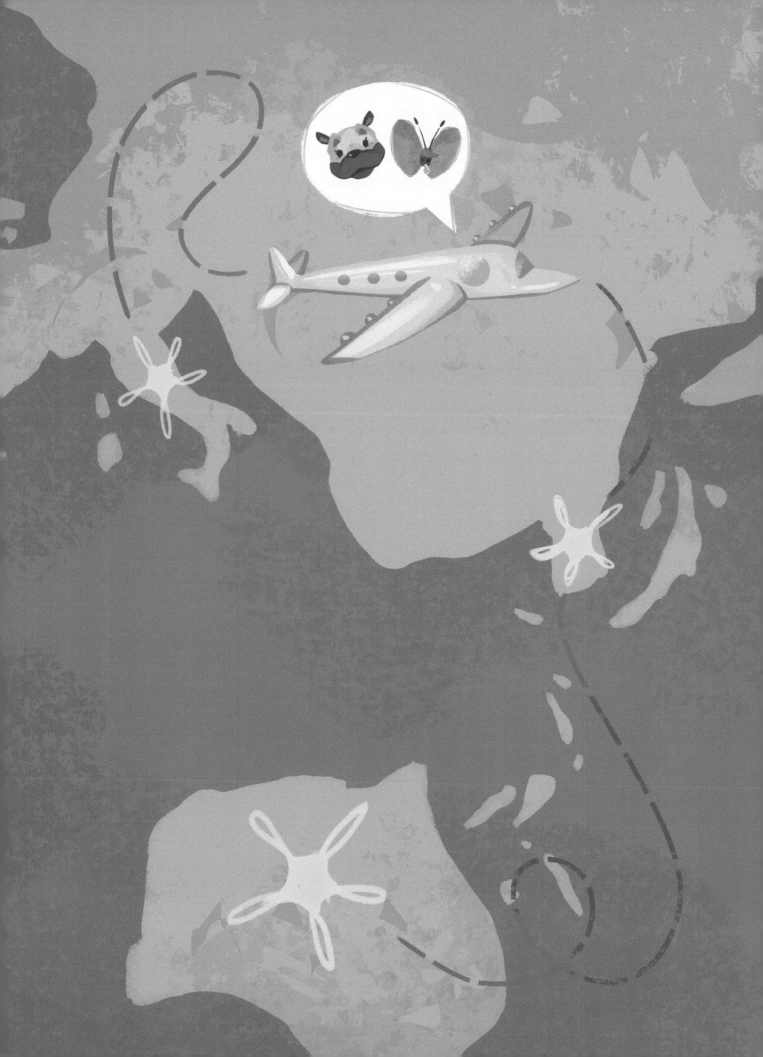

Bodybuilding Champion

Because of all her hard work and focus,

NELLY PUG

won many 1st place titles and even
earned best bodybuilder in the whole
U.S.A. for one of the leagues.

NELLY PUG

always brought her husband, Ryan Pug,
to watch her. He would bark and howl for
her louder than any of the other dogs.

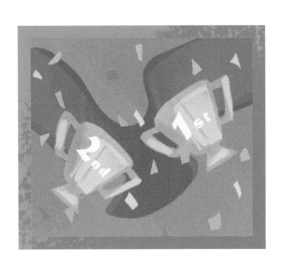

NELLY PUG

now had a big picture on the gym wall of herself. She had become a bodybuilding star. She had dreamed about her goals, worked for her goals, and achieved her goals. Sometimes that meant watching less T.V. and playing less computer games. Being a pug bodybuilder made her exercise and eat protein and vegetables, not junk food. She had to go to bed on time too.

Coach Eddie Monarch helped

NELLY PUG

grow beautiful, natural muscles.
She was an example of being healthy
to all her dog friends and family.

Health Benefits of Physical Activity

FOR CHILDREN

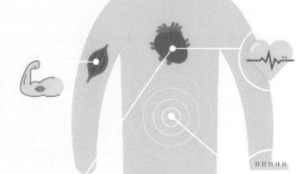

Academic Performance

Improves attention and memory

Brain Health

Reduces risk of depression

Muscular Fitness

Builds strong muscles and endurance

Heart and Lung Health

Improves blood pressure and aerobic fitness

Cardiometabolic Health

Helps maintain normal blood sugar levels

Long-term Health

Reduces risk of several chronic diseases, including type 2 diabetes and obesity

Healthy Weight

Helps regulate body weight and reduce body fat

Bone Strength

Strengthens bones

ACTIVE PEOPLE, HEALTHY NATION

Source: *Physical Activity Guidelines for Americans, 2nd edition*

To learn more, visit: https://www.cdc.gov/physicalactivity/basics/adults/health-benefits-of-physical-activity-for-children.html

October 2021

CHILDHOOD NUTRITION FACTS
HEALTHY SCHOOLS | CDC

Children need to eat healthy in order to grow and develop properly and to prevent poor health conditions. Healthy eating can help children to also maintain a healthy body weight. The Dietary Guidelines for Americans, 2020–2025 recommends that people aged 2 years or older follow a healthy eating lifestyle to include:

A variety of fruits and vegetables.

1. Whole grains.
2. Fat-free and low-fat dairy products.
3. A variety of protein foods.
4. Oils.

Healthy eating can prevent and help avoid the following:

1. High blood pressure.
2. Type 2 diabetes.
3. Cancer.
4. Cavities and dental problems.
5. Heart disease.
6. Iron deficiency.
7. Osteoporosis.

Here is a great recipe for children to enjoy snacks. Try taking a muffin pan and placing servings of various healthy snacks in each cup. Ideas include fruits, whole-grain crackers and/or pretzels, and vegetables. This makes a wonderful, colorful display of healthy portions children can choose from. This is a great example of planning ahead for nutrition during the week and demonstrates to children what true servings sizes/portions look like. This visual representation can be learned and used when independently eating. Each day the child gets to pick 1 or 2 of the choices and return to the pan the next day for what is left (of course make sure to store in the refrigerator or properly). What a fun way to learn about healthy eating and maybe even make one of the cups for their pug to have a snack too 😊

15 reasNONS
TO GeT a PUG

1. Pugs have squishy faces.

2. Pugs have wrinkles.

3. Pugs will cuddle all day.

4. Pugs have curly tails that look like a cinnamon roll.

5. Pugs look like baked potatos.

6. Pugs snore.

7. Pugs love children.

8. Pugs tilt their heads when you talk to them.

9. Pugs love healthy treats and food.

10. Pugs are loyal.

11. Pugs are funny.

12. Pugs like walks.

13. Pugs like car rides.

14. Pugs are friendly with other pugs.

15. Pugs just want to be by you all day long.

about the author

Dr. Megan Johnson McCullough, EdD, is the owner of Every BODY's Fit (fitness studio) in Oceanside, CA. She is a Doctor of Health and Human Performance and is a Drug and Alcohol Fitness Recovery Specialist. Dr. McCullough is also a world champion professional natural bodybuilder, fitness model, and has 4 other books she has published with Palmetto and 2 more cookbooks she has written about metabolism. Other credentials Dr. McCullough has held include Master Trainer (National Academy of Sports Medicine), Personal Trainer (National Exercise & Sports Trainers Association), Group Exercise Instructor in Aqua, Cycle, Yoga, and Zumba (Aerobics and Fitness Association of America), Corrective Exercise Specialist, Fitness Nutrition Specialist, Senior Fitness Specialist, Wellness Coach, and Lifestyle and Weight Management Specialist. She is happily married to her husband, Carl, and loves her two pugs, Steve Nash and Scottie Pippen. Dr. McCullough also has a research book currently in publication and has released a cell phone application called Fit PACE for persons in addiction recovery to incorporate exercise to help maintain sobriety.

Photo credit Ben Yosef,
International Physique League

To connect with Dr. McCullough you can find more information here:

Website: https://www.everybodysfitoceanside.com
Instagram @dr.megan_everybodysfit
FB: https://www.facebook.com/megan.johnson.374549
YouTube: https://www.youtube.com/fitlifeeverybodysfit
Amazon: https://www.bit.ly/MeganJohnsonMcCullough
Linked In: www.linkedin.com/in/megan-johnson-mccullough-1b603a80

Ingram Content Group UK Ltd.
Milton Keynes UK
UKHW051534190323
418651UK00008B/83